Bull Rider

by Marilyn Halvorson

All of a sudden a flash of red caught my
eye way up in the stands. Someone in
a red shirt up there, watching. Nobody
was supposed to be around. If Mom
found out what I was doing I was
dead.

It took maybe half a second for all
that to flash through my mind. But that
was enough. In that half second I lost
my concentration.

And in that half second Rhino
stopped spinning to the right and
started spinning left. I tried to shift my
balance and go with him, but it was too
late. I was losing it. . . .

Other books by Marilyn Halvorson

Cowboys Don't Cry
Let It Go
Nobody Said It Would Be Easy
Dare

series **MARILYN HALVORSON**

2000

Wapiti regional library

Bull
Rider

Jenna

Foster

9001611

Collier Macmillan Canada, Inc.

Collier Macmillan Canada, Inc.
1200 Eglinton Ave. E., Suite 200
Don Mills, Ontario M3C 3N1

ISBN 0-02-953547-6

GENERAL EDITOR: Paul Kropp
SERIES EDITOR: Sandra Gulland
TITLE EDITOR: Glenn Woods
DESIGNER: Brant Cowie
ILLUSTRATOR: Greg Ruhl
COVER PHOTOGRAPH: Paterson Photographic

1 2 3 4 5 6 9 3 9 2 9 1 9 0 8 9
Printed and bound in Canada

CANADIAN CATALOGUING IN PUBLICATION DATA
Halvorson, Marilyn
  Bull rider

(Series 2000)
ISBN 0-02-953547-6

I. Title.   II. Series.

PS8565.A48B84 1989   JC813'.54   C89-093734-6
PZ7.H34Bu 1989

To my mom, who taught me to love books. And to Ruth and Art, whose faith and friendship has seen me through some hard times.

CONTENTS

CHAPTER 1

I was sitting at the kitchen table when Mom came in. "Hi, Layne," she said, setting down a bag of groceries. "Doing your homework already?" she asked with a grin. "You sure you're feeling all right?"

Any other time I would have grinned back. Mom nags me so much about homework that it's kind of a joke between us. But this time I didn't crack a smile. I was too nervous. "It's not homework," I said slowly, looking up at her.

She shrugged and crammed some lettuce into the fridge. "No?" she said, only half listening. "What is it then?"

I swallowed. "An entry form for the rodeo next month," I said, and watched her grin fade.

I knew she'd be like this. She had been like this the other two times I had tried. But it

wouldn't be quite the same this time. Because this time I wasn't backing down.

Mom slowly closed the fridge and came over to the table. She never took her eyes off me until she picked up the entry form. Then she glanced at it, crumpled it up, and threw it on the table. "No, Layne," she said in a tight voice. Her eyes met mine again. "Not the bull riding. You know how I feel about that."

"Yeah," I answered angrily, "and you know how I feel about it too."

"I don't care how you feel," Mom shot back. "All I know is that I watched a bull kill my husband and there's no way I'll watch one kill my son."

I stood up fast—and almost knocked the table over. "That won't happen—"

"You bet it won't happen," Mom cut in before I could finish. "The answer is no!" She grabbed her jacket and headed for the door.

"You can't stop me," I said in a flat voice. That got her attention, and she spun right around. Mom and I have more in common than our brown hair and blue eyes. Our tempers match, too. Her eyes flashed angrily, but before she could say anything I cut her off. "Mom, give me a break," I said. "I'm almost seventeen."

Mom laughed—but it wasn't a happy laugh. "Right, Layne, *almost*. Just ten more months till your birthday." Then, in a voice hard as steel, she added, "And I've got news for you. As long as you're living in this house, I *can* stop you. And don't you ever forget it."

I looked her straight in the eye. "If that's the way it's gotta be," I said, "I'll get out of this house. But, I'm gonna ride."

Right away I realized I'd backed myself into a corner. You couldn't push my mom like that and get away with it. What if she called my bluff? Leaving home was the last thing I wanted to do.

Mom and I stood there for a minute, glaring at each other. Was she really tough enough to kick me out if I entered the bull riding?

Suddenly she glanced at her watch, gave a gasp, and ran for the door. I was glad there wasn't time to finish this fight right now.

Mom's a nurse and works the late shift at the hospital in Greentree. It's hard to hold a steady job and keep the ranch going, too. But she has no choice. The ranch isn't a great money maker—especially when you've got a family to support.

I heard her start the Dodge and burn out of the driveway. If I spun that much gravel I'd hear about it.

I picked up my entry form and carefully smoothed it out. It was in rough shape but I could still use it.

"Cool move, Hot Shot." A voice from behind me made me jump. It was Terror, of course, my kid sister. Her real name is Tara, but if you knew her you'd understand the nickname. I hadn't even known she was in the house. Knowing her, I'd bet she hadn't missed that scene between me and Mom.

"What's that supposed to mean?" I snarled back at her.

"Don't you think Mom's got enough problems? She sure doesn't need you getting her all upset."

Great. That was all I needed—a free guilt trip. "Get off my case, Terr," I snapped. I pushed past her and headed for my room.

I changed into an old shirt. What I had in mind was real hard on clothes. As I turned to go out, the newspaper clipping on the wall caught my eye. It had been there so long it was yellow, but the headline still stood out. ONE RIDE AWAY FROM A CHAMPIONSHIP.

The picture was clear, too. My dad, grinning from ear to ear right after he scored an eighty-five at the National Finals. It was the last ride he ever finished. On his next bull he got his hand caught in the rope. By the time they got him loose it was too late. He was trampled so bad he never woke up.

That happened six years ago, but it still seems like yesterday. I was ten years old and my whole world fell apart. With Dad gone there was a big hollow space inside of me that I thought nothing would ever fill. I used to lie awake at night thinking about him. About how bad he'd wanted that championship and how close he'd come to getting it.

And, slowly an idea had begun to take shape. Dad would never win the championship, but maybe his son could do it for him.

14

I've been working on it ever since, but it hasn't been easy. Oh, I've done a lot of steer riding. I was already entering the Boys Steer Riding before Dad died and I kept at it. Mom didn't mind that. Steer riding isn't all that dangerous. But I'm too old for that now and riding bulls is a lot different. The only way you can learn to ride bulls is the hard way—by riding them. And that's where Jana Kelvin comes into the picture.

I stuffed my shirt tail into my jeans and headed outside. I didn't make it. Halfway through the kitchen Terror caught up to me. "You goin' down to Kelvin's arena again, Layne?"

I turned around. "What's it to you?" I said angrily. She wasn't supposed to know I was going there.

"Lots," she said. "Cause, if you are you can hook the trailer on and take Rambo and me with you. I want to practise barrel racing him."

Terror and Rambo. The perfect pair. Rambo was her horse and the name fit him just right. All great body and not enough brains to come in out of the rain. He might have the build for a barrel racing horse, but I didn't think he'd ever make it. He was too pig-headed. He'd just as soon run right over the barrels as do the figure-eight around them.

Anyhow, there was no way I was going to haul that outlaw horse anywhere. Last time he was in the trailer he almost kicked a hole through it. Besides, I didn't want Terror along any more than I wanted her horse.

"Why should I take you?" I said. "What have you ever done for me?" After that run-in with Mom I didn't feel like being anything but miserable.

Terror's eyes narrowed. "I've done plenty of things for you," she said angrily. "But you better worry about what I'm gonna do *to* you if you don't take me along."

"Oh, wow," I sneered. "You're scarin' me to death."

She shrugged. "O.K, if that's the way you want it." She started to walk away.

I let her walk a dozen steps before I broke down. Calling Terror's bluff could be dangerous.

"Well," I yelled after her. "What *are* you gonna do?"

She tossed her head. "Tell Mom that Jana Kelvin's letting you practise on her dad's bulls," she said.

We went out and loaded Rambo.

CHAPTER 2

We pulled up beside Kelvin's arena. Jana was waiting for us. I leaned out of the window of the truck. "Hi, Jana," I said.

"Hi, Layne," she said with that great smile of hers. "Come to break your neck again?"

"Sure. Why not?" I answered.

Jack Kelvin, Jana's dad, is a rodeo stock contractor. That means he supplies the broncs and bulls for the rodeos. This was about the fourth time I'd been over to the Kelvin's arena. Jana let me ride bulls that were still too young to be used in rodeos.

"O.K. if I take a few runs around the barrels?" Terror asked.

Jana smiled. "Sure, Terr, help yourself. Help me chase a couple of bulls in first?"

The girls got on their horses and rode into the corral behind the arena. I picked up my riggin' bag and walked inside the big building. I opened the gate that led into the chutes.

A minute later three bulls came trotting in. I had ridden the first two. They were young, just going on two years old, and not very big yet.

But it was the third one that caught my eye. He was black and had only one shiny black horn. That bull was no baby. He was full-grown and, under that loose, Brahma hide, rippling with muscle.

Jana came riding up on Magpie, her pinto. "Sorry," she said. "I didn't mean to get old Rhino in here. He just saw the gate open and charged right in."

"Rhino?" I said.

"Yeah. The black guy. He broke his other horn off a couple of years ago and he's been Rhino ever since."

"Where'd he come from?" I asked. "I've never seen him before."

Jana laughed. "Oh, you know Dad. He's always trading. He just got Rhino from a stock contractor down south. He didn't take him to the High River rodeo because he wants him to settle down a little first." She started to turn her horse away. "I'll get him out of here," she said. "Which one do you want in the chute?"

"Him," I said.

"Who? Rhino?"

"Yeah," I said, nodding toward the big black bull.

Jana brought Magpie to a sudden stop. "Hey, wait a minute—" she began, but I didn't let her finish.

"Come on, Jana, you know I'm not gonna learn any more from those young ones. They're not tough enough."

Jana looked doubtful. "Yeah, but what if Rhino's *too* tough?"

I gave her a grin. "Then he's gonna win and I'm gonna lose. Let me try him, Jana. He looks like he's got the right attitude."

"He looks like he'll eat you for breakfast," Terror's voice cut in cheerfully from behind me.

I turned around and glared at her. "Don't get your hopes up, Terror. I'm gonna ride this sucker." Then I picked up my rope and headed for the chute.

The first thing I learned about Rhino was that he was a chute fighter. He wasn't even planning to let me get my rope on him. Every time I touched him he snorted and stomped around like he had a hide full of hornets.

I climbed up on the side of the chute. Jana was already on the other side getting the flank strap ready. Just like the name says, the flank strap goes around the bull's flanks. It's there to make him mad—it tickles him just enough to make him really want to buck.

We got the strap on O.K., but the rope was even harder. The rope goes just behind the front legs. It's pretty important because it's all the rider has to hang on to.

Rhino finally stood still long enough for me to swing the rope under him. Jana caught it on the other side and pulled it up snug. She brought the tail of the rope up and tucked it through the handhold while I put my glove on my riding hand.

I carefully eased myself down onto Rhino's back. That's when I felt the raw power of his muscles. This was going to be some ride! I wondered what Dad would have thought of him.

Jana's voice brought my mind back to the present. "Hurry up, Layne. Get that resin worked into your rope. Rhino isn't going to stand for much more."

Jana was right. Rhino wanted out. Quickly I slid my gloved hand up and down the rope. The resin had warmed up and was sticky enough to keep my hand from slipping. I was almost ready.

"I don't know about this, Layne," Jana said, sounding worried. "Rhino's a pretty rank bull. What if he unloads you and then goes for you?"

I had sort of been wondering the same thing, but now I just shrugged. "He's not so bad," I said. "He's just a chute fighter. He'll be O.K. when he gets outside. Besides," I added with a grin, "he's not gonna unload me."

Jana raised an eyebrow and said, "Think you're good, don't you?"

"I know it."

She laughed at that one. My macho act

never impressed Jana much. It didn't seem to impress the bull either. Right then he gave a sudden lunge that almost mashed my leg against the gate. I settled down and paid attention.

Concentration. That's what it was all about. Dad used to say you rode bulls as much with your brain as with your body.

O.K., Dad, I thought. *Watch this.* I slid up on the rope, toes out, chin in. I took a deep breath and nodded. "Let him out!"

Jana jerked the gate open and got out of the way, fast.

Rhino exploded out of that chute and the whole world started spinning. In fact, the whole world disappeared. Everything was gone except for that bull and me. From what seemed like a million miles away I could hear a voice yelling, "Feet! Feet!" Somehow my mind took it in. Jana. Telling me to keep my feet in. Right, feet in. Sit up straight. I tried to remember all the stuff Dad had told me. But it had been a long time ago.

All of a sudden a flash of red caught my eye way up in the stands. Someone in a red shirt

up there, watching. Nobody was supposed to be around. If Mom found out what I was doing I was dead.

It took maybe half a second for all that to flash through my mind. But that was enough. In that half second I lost my concentration.

And in that half second Rhino stopped spinning to the right and started spinning left. I tried to shift my balance and go with him, but it was too late. I was losing it . . . .

CHAPTER 3

I hit the ground hard and got the wind knocked out of me. Then a feeling of relief swept over me. Rhino had thrown me, all right, but he'd thrown me clear. I hadn't got tangled up. Even as I was thinking that, I was scrambling to my feet. When you get thrown off a bull you don't wait around to talk it over with him.

I was only half standing up when he hit me. I caught one glimpse of black coming at me and then I was flying through the air. I hit the ground face down and started to get up again. I had to get out of there, fast. But it was too late. Before I could get up off my knees, Rhino's head slammed me back down. I knew I wasn't going to get away from him. It was time to play turtle.

I buried my head in my arms and pulled my knees up to my belly. Then Rhino was after me again. I could feel the heat of his breath and smell the scent of hay on it. It smelled kind of good. *Being killed by a bull sure beat being killed by a bear,* I thought dimly. They say bears have rotten breath.

But they don't have horns, I reminded myself. I felt Rhino's horn scrape across my ribs like a dull knife. If he kept that up he was going to do some damage. I was surprised at how calm I felt. It was weird. I felt like I wasn't part of what was going on.

Suddenly I heard someone yell, real close, and Rhino stopped trying to grind me into the dirt. I uncurled enough to look up. What I saw *really* scared me. Terror was standing right in front of the bull waving her jacket in his face and screaming at him. Before I could move, the bull gave a low bellow and went for Terror. Like lightning she jumped aside. He went charging by, tearing the jacket out of her hands.

Rhino turned around, snorting and pawing the ground. But by then Jana was there. She came charging up behind Rhino on her horse, swinging a big wicked whip in her hand. The

end of it caught Rhino's glossy black rump with a loud smack. The bull gave a startled bawl and instantly forgot Terror and me. He took off for the gate with Jana and Magpie right behind him.

I propped myself up on one elbow and spit out some dirt. Then I looked up at Terror. She was standing there grinning like she was in her right mind.

I glared at her. "Of all the stupid, pea-brained, air-headed . . . ," I began. But I was still crunching sand between my teeth. I spit out some more and tried again. "What were you tryin' to do? Get killed?" I yelled. My voice came out kind of shaky. Actually, I was starting to feel sort of shaky all over.

Terror just shrugged. "Look who's talking. *You're* the one bleeding."

"I am?" I said, surprised. I'd been too busy taking a strip off her to worry about me. But now I looked down and saw the big rip in the side of my shirt. The torn edges of the denim were slowly turning dark red.

Now that I thought about it, my side was hurting some, too. I pulled out my shirt tail and checked the damage. There was a long, bloody groove across my ribs—thanks to Rhino's one sharp horn. It was a messy-looking cut, but not deep enough to be serious.

I looked up, ready to tell Terror that the cut was nothing. That's when I saw a man walking slowly across the arena. My first reaction was anger. This was the guy in the red shirt, the one I'd seen up in the stands. He was the reason I had lost my concentration. If it hadn't been for him I would have ridden Rhino—maybe.

The man was close enough to recognize now. I felt a sinking feeling in the pit of my stomach. It was Chase Kincaid, Jana's grandfather, and I knew he was going to have a few questions.

Jana rode over to see what was happening. She and her grandfather got there at about the same time. For a minute nobody said anything. Chase just stood there glaring at all three of us with those pale old eagle eyes of his. I stood there scuffing my boots in the dirt and waited for him to start yelling.

Finally I heard Jana take a deep breath. "I, uh, thought you went to town with Mom. But I guess you didn't 'cause you're, uh, here. . . ."

Shut up, Jana, I said silently. When you're in this deep, every word just gets you in deeper. But Jana kept right on talking. "Uh, Gramps, this is a friend of mine, Layne McQueen. You know, he lives—"

Chase cut her off. "Course I know who he is," he growled. "I remember the day he was born. Never saw a man prouder than Jeff McQueen was that day."

I stood there staring at him. The last thing I expected was for him to start talking about Dad. But I guess they had known each other pretty well. Dad used to talk about Chase a lot. Chase had been a bull rider, too, when he was young. Not just *a* bull rider, I remembered. According to Dad, he had been the best.

But just when I was hoping that Chase had got lost somewhere in the past, his eagle eyes focussed on me. "But what I don't know," he said slowly, "is what you think you're tryin' to do here."

I swallowed hard and prepared to die. "I was practising," I said weakly.

Chase gave kind of a snort. "Well, from what I could see, Lord knows you could use the practice."

I felt my face turning red.

"Don't suppose you ever thought of just walking up and asking when you want to use something?" he went on. "Or is sneaking around your style?"

I had that coming. I made myself look him in the eye. "I should have known better," I said, wishing I was dead and buried.

Chase nodded. "Yeah," he said. He thought a minute. Then he gave me a puzzled look. "So," he said at last, "if you're so all-fired set on riding bulls, why don't you just sign up for the next rodeo?"

I hated answering that question. I studied my boots. "My mom won't let me," I muttered. It made me feel like I was too young to cross the street alone.

Chase thought that over for a minute. What he said next surprised me. "On account of

33

what happened to your dad?" he asked, his voice gentle.

I nodded. "How'd you know?" I asked, giving Jana an accusing look. She was about the only person who knew why I couldn't ride bulls at rodeos. I hadn't expected her to tell anybody.

But I guess Chase didn't need an explanation from Jana. "I can see that," he said. "I don't blame your mom." *Sure,* I thought. *He'd be on her side.* But then he added, "Don't blame you either." I was still taking that in when I made the mistake of reaching over to rub my sore ribs. Chase noticed the blood.

"Cut you up a little, huh?" he said. I nodded. Chase stepped forward for a closer look. "Let's see," he ordered.

He leaned over and inspected the cut. Then he reached into his pocket and came out with a jack-knife. I almost backed up. What was this? Instant surgery while-you-wait? But it was just my shirt tail he was after. He cut off a chunk. "Shirt's done for anyway," he said. He pulled a handkerchief out of his pocket and

slapped it on the cut. "Here, hold this," he ordered. I did and he wrapped the strip of shirt around me to hold the handkerchief in place. Then he jerked it real tight. I winced as it bit into my ribs.

Chase gave me a sharp look. "You all right?" he asked.

I nodded. "Yeah, I'm O.K." I said. Bull-riding injuries come in two kinds. If you're moving, you're O.K. If you're not, they get the stretcher.

I was definitely O.K.

CHAPTER 4

There was no point in hanging around any longer. It was only going to be a matter of time before Chase told Jana's parents and they told Mom. I could feel his eyes still on me as I turned away. Head down, I started walking out to the truck. Jana fell into step beside me.

"You look kind of pale," she said. "You sure you feel O.K., Layne?"

"Yeah," I began, meaning to say, *It was nothin'*. But then I looked into Jana's big, brown eyes. They were soft and full of concern—and real pretty. I began to take a turn for the worse. "Well," I said, trying to sound brave, but in pain. "I guess I could be better. I'm kinda shook."

It worked. Jana reached out and put her arm around my waist. "Here," she said, "lean on me." I did and we walked slowly over to the truck. I was feeling better already.

Terror walked beside us, leading the horses. She caught my eye. The look on her face said that she was ready to either laugh or throw up. Sometimes my kid sister sees through me all too well.

Luckily, it was right then that Rambo decided to reach over and take a bite out of Magpie's neck. Magpie went straight up and Terror had all she could handle sorting out that little rodeo. At least it got her mind off my business. Maybe old Rambo really did have his good side.

We got him loaded without too much trouble. Then I started to climb in on the driver's side. Terror stopped me. "Hey, Layne, since you're feeling 'kinda shook', maybe I should drive." The look on her face was halfway between hopeful and teasing.

"Dream on, kid," I said, sliding behind the wheel. "You're only twelve."

Terror shrugged. "Never hurts to try," she said, walking around to the other side.

Jana stood leaning on my door. "I'm really sorry, Layne," she said softly. "What's your mom gonna say?"

I sighed. "Don't ask."

Jana just stood there giving me that worried look for a minute. Then, all of a sudden, she leaned over and gave me a quick kiss. "Good luck, Layne," she said.

"Oh, gross," Terror muttered and I felt my face start to burn.

"Thanks, Jana," I said, real low.

As we drove out of the yard I got one last glimpse of Chase. He was leaning on the fence watching us go. I couldn't read the expression on his face.

We drove in silence for a while. Finally I glanced over at Terror. "So," I said wearily, "I suppose you can't wait to blab the whole story to Mom."

She gave me a narrow-eyed look. "Isn't that what you'd expect from a stupid, pea-brained, air-headed—"

I cut her off. "O.K., O.K., I didn't mean that stuff. But you had me so scared . . . ."

Terror fluffed up like an insulted cat. "*I* had *you* scared!" she squeaked. "If *somebody* hadn't done *something*, that bull would have made hamburger out of you."

I couldn't come up with a real good answer to that. I couldn't think of much of anything to say at all. Except for one thing. And it wasn't going to be easy.

"Uh, Terr?" She looked at me. "What you did, about the bull, I mean, uh, thanks. I, uh, appreciate it." I could feel my face turning red. I haven't had much practice talking nice to Terror.

Terror hadn't had much practice hearing me say thank you either. For once she was stuck for words. Finally she gave me a sideways look. "Aw that was nothin'," she muttered gruffly.

For a long while neither of us said anything. Then, as we started up our driveway, she turned to me. "You never know," she said. "Maybe Chase won't tell."

"Sure," I said tiredly. "And maybe I'm Arnold Schwarzenegger."

After supper I made a half-hearted stab at doing my homework. Terror turned the TV on, but I decided to go to bed early. I was feeling like I'd been run over by a bull. And that was nothing compared to how I expected to feel when Mom found out. I didn't think I'd be able to sleep, but the next thing I knew it was morning.

I woke up to the sound of a quick knock on my bedroom door. I blinked, tried to sit up fast, and got a stab of pain through my ribs for my trouble. The door opened and Mom came in, gathering up my dirty clothes to wash.

"Mornin', Sunshine," she said brightly. She threw me a teasing grin over her shoulder. It was an old joke between us. Sunshine was one name that didn't exactly fit me first thing in the morning.

"Mornin'," I muttered sleepily. She probably thought she'd won our last little set-to. Now she wanted to show that there were no hard feelings about it. *O.K., Mom, I* thought. *No hard feelings. But you still haven't won.*

Right in the middle of that thought, I saw something that brought my attention back to the present real fast. My denim shirt, the one with the rip and the blood, was lying crumpled up in the corner. It was right where

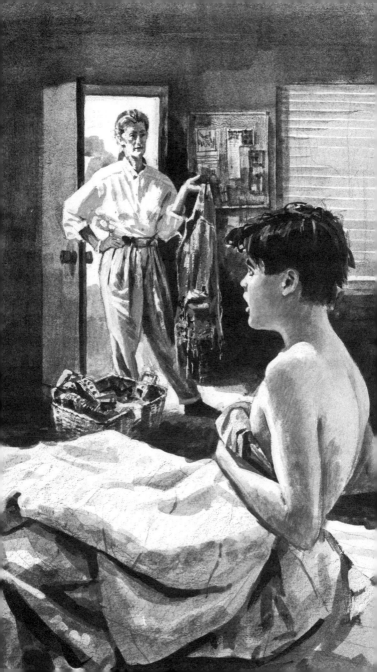

I'd tossed it last night. I'd been planning to get rid of it first thing in the morning, but now it was too late. Sure enough, Mom spotted it.

She shook her head. "You are some housekeeper, Layne," she muttered as she bent over to pick it up. "Ever think of putting your dirty clothes in the hamper?" She gave the shirt a shake and started to throw it in the basket. Then she took another look.

When she looked up at me there was a little crease between her eyes. That usually means that she's either thinking hard or getting mad. Sometimes both.

"Now what . . . ?" she began. I wasn't sure if she expected an answer from me. She didn't get one anyway. Like the cops always say on TV, "You have the right to remain silent. Anything you say may be held against you. . . ."

"Did you have rugby practice after school yesterday?" she asked, sounding disgusted.

That was the last question I expected and it caught me off guard. "Uh, yeah," I answered honestly. I'd been late getting home because of it.

"For two cents I'd phone up that coach of yours and give him a piece of my mind," she said. "This is the third shirt you've ruined this month. Look at this," she went on. "Blood even. You're always getting scratched up. That rugby is too violent for school kids."

I said a mental thank you to Mr. Bowlen and his killer rugby practices. He didn't know it but he had just saved my neck—temporarily at least.

Then I realized that Mom was still muttering on about the rugby. The way she was going on I was afraid she actually would phone Mr. Bowlen.

I sat up a little straighter, making sure to take the blanket with me. I still had on Chase's homemade bandage. Mom wouldn't buy the idea that it had come from the school's first-aid kit. "You know," I said innocently, "I'm getting kinda sick of rugby. Maybe I'll take up a different sport."

Mom gave me a suspicious look. I guess I'd never given up that easy before in my life. But, luckily, she was too busy to worry about it. She stuffed the shirt in the basket and headed for the door. "Good idea, Layne," she said over her shoulder. "Anything would be an improvement."

I smiled as she went out the door. *Anything, Mom?* I said silently.

CHAPTER 5

I didn't have a great day at school. With everything that had happened I'd forgot to do my homework. That got me a detention. But that was nothing compared to what would be waiting for me when I got home. I figured by then Chase would have spilled the beans to Mom.

I had to walk home, but we live not too far out of town so that wasn't so bad. It was about four-thirty when I turned into our lane. I half expected Mom to ambush me in the front yard.

I opened the door and walked into the house. Mom wasn't there either. Just Terror eating peanut butter with a spoon and watching "The Young and the Restless." I dumped my books on the table. "Where's Mom?" I asked.

Terror ignored me until the couple on the

screen finished kissing. Then she set down the peanut butter and looked at me. "Out," she said, helpfully.

"I know she's out. Out where?"

Terror shrugged. "Checking on the cows, I think." Then, acting real innocent, she asked, "Why do you want to know?"

"You know why I want to know," I shot back impatiently. "So what's she acting like? Did she find out?"

Another shrug. "She didn't say anything."

The show ended. Terror turned the TV off. "Oh, yeah," she said casually, "you had a phone call."

"I did? Who was it, Jana?"

"Nope."

"Well, who?" I asked, my voice rising. I could wring her neck when she acts like this.

"Chase Kincaid," she said, giving me a sideways look.

That hit me like a punch in the stomach. "Chase! Did he talk to Mom?"

Terror shook her head. "She was outside. Anyway, it was you he wanted."

For a minute I just stood there, trying to

take that in. I wondered if this was good news or bad. Before I could decide, Terror went on. "He left you a message."

"Yeah? What'd he say?"

"He said to show up at the arena tonight at seven."

"And bring Mom?" I asked, kind of sickly.

Terror shook her head. "No."

I stared at her for a minute, wondering if she was making it all up. "Well," I demanded, "what else did he say?"

Terror picked up an apple and bit into it with a loud crunch. "Nothin'," she said, heading for the door. Then she looked back over her shoulder. "Except that I could come too if I wanted." She opened the door and then stopped. "So," she asked, "are you gonna show up?"

I sighed. "I don't think I've got a choice," I said. One thing was for sure. Whatever game Chase was playing, he was holding all the aces.

Mom came in after a while. She just acted normal so I tried to do the same. Whatever Chase had in mind, he hadn't told her yet. I wasn't looking forward to facing him, but the suspense was killing me.

At 6:45 I was in the truck. Terror was, too. I didn't much want her along, but I wasn't in any position to give her static.

The first thing I noticed when we drove into Kelvin's yard was that all the vehicles were gone. Jana's mom and dad must be away again. Jana was there, though. She came out to meet us.

"Hi, Jana," I said nervously. "What's goin' on?"

Jana looked as confused as I felt. "Beats me," she said. "Gramps just mentioned that you might be coming over. That's all he said."

I didn't get a chance to ask any more questions. Chase was strolling over from the arena. I noticed he limped a little. Most old bull riders do.

I got out of the truck and stood there, waiting. Chase gave me a long, measuring look. "How you feelin'?" he asked at last.

That wasn't what I was expecting. For a second my mind went blank. He'd called me

over here to ask about my health? "I'm O.K.,"
I said, kind of sheepishly.

Chase nodded. "Good," he said. "Where's
your bull rope?"

I stared at him. "In the truck," I said. I
always kept it behind the seat so Mom
wouldn't find it. Was he going to take it away
from me so I couldn't sneak any more rides?

"Get it," Chase said.

As I was getting it out he turned to Jana.
"Go and saddle up a horse." He nodded
toward Terror. "And get one for the
bullfighter here too," he added.

"O.K, Gramps," Jana said, giving him an
unbelieving look. "Come on, Terr."

The look on Terror's face almost made me
grin. She doesn't usually take orders. She did
it this time, though.

"Here," I muttered, holding my bull rope
out to him. I was remembering how long it
had taken me to save the money to buy it.

Chase didn't take the rope. He just gave me
a scornful look. "What're you givin' me that
for?" he asked. "Think I'm about to climb on
a bull at my age?"

I stared at him. "No, but you said—"

He cut me off. "I said get it. Now you've got it."

Without another word he limped off toward the arena. I just stood there until he threw me an impatient glance over his shoulder. "Well," he asked, "you comin' or ain't you?"

Chase had kept me off balance from the minute I'd driven in. I was getting kind of sick of being jerked around like a lassoed calf. But, I followed him.

Just as I caught up to him Jana and Terror rode up. "Now what, Gramps?" Jana asked.

"Go run in a couple of the young bulls," Chase ordered.

Jana just stared at him.

"Got a hearing problem?" Chase asked, giving her his "eagle" look.

Suddenly, Jana grinned. "No sir!" she yelled. She and Terror both took off at a gallop.

That left Chase and me. "You gonna tell me what's goin' on?" I asked. I matched his glare with one of my own.

Chase brought a can of Copenhagen out of his back pocket and helped himself to a chew. Then he nodded at the rope that was still in my hand. "Suppose I took that thing away from you, told your mom what you'd been up to, and told you to stay away from the bulls. What would you do then?"

"I'd get another rope, and I'd find another place to practise. And if Mom couldn't handle that, I'd find another place to live." The words just came out.

It was the first time I realized how important this was to me. But, once I'd said it, I knew I meant every word of it.

Chase nodded. "That's what I figured," he said gruffly, but his lined face had softened a little. "So you might just as well do it right as wrong."

Slowly, I began to understand. "You mean you're gonna *teach* me?" I asked.

"Depends if you're teachable," Chase said. Something pretty close to a grin was creeping across his face.

I didn't know what to say. My dad had said Chase was the best bull rider he'd ever known. It was like Christmas had just come seven months early. "I'll learn," I promised. "I'll do whatever you say."

Chase nodded. "We'll see," he said.

Then, as the bulls came trotting in, I had to ask one last question. "Chase?"

"Yeah?"

"You're taking a big chance for me. Why?"

Chase thought a minute. "It's tough bein' a kid," he said at last. "You want to do something, and nobody thinks you're old enough to handle it." He turned and started walking toward the chutes. Then, over his shoulder he added, "There's only one thing worse. That's bein' so old nobody thinks you can do anything."

He kept on walking, but I had my answer.

CHAPTER 6

I watched as Chase picked out the bull he wanted. I didn't understand his choice. It was a pretty good-sized bull for its age, all right, big-boned and well-muscled. But, from his red and white colour and calm disposition, I'd bet this bull was more Hereford than Brahma.

I climbed up on the fence beside Chase. "I've ridden him before," I said. "He's not much of a bull."

"So, ride him again," he said. Something in his voice told me not to argue.

We got the rigging on the bull and I slid on. Chase leaned over me making adjustments and giving advice. He pulled the rope snug for me. Then I started to weave it in and out of my fingers like I always did. Suddenly, Chase grabbed my wrist like an eagle's claw would grab a rabbit. "What do you think you're doin'?" he asked in a voice as hard as his grip.

I just stared at him, stunned. "What do you mean?" I asked.

He still didn't let go of my wrist. "Don't you know any better than to use a suicide wrap?"

"Suicide wrap?" I repeated.

Chase nodded grimly. "Yeah. That's what it's called and that's what it is. You fall off wrong with your hand tied in like that and you're dead. Whoever taught you that should be shot. Who was it, anyhow?" he demanded, his eyes burning into me.

I looked back at him defiantly. "My dad," I said.

There was a silence. Then Chase nodded. "It figures," he said, wearily.

I almost shot back an angry reply. I didn't know what his comment was supposed to mean. But I didn't like it.

Nobody put down my dad when I was around. But then the truth began to sink in. Dad had always ridden with a "suicide wrap"—and now Dad was dead. In all the years since the accident I'd never really put it all together.

Chase's voice interrupted my thoughts. "Yeah," he said. "Some guys figure that the extra grip it gives you is worth the risk. But as long as you're working with me you ain't gonna be one of them." Before I could argue he was running the rope through my gloved hand. Then he folded the tail of the rope back over—but not between my fingers.

I flexed my hand. It felt funny that way. I gave Chase an angry look. He ignored it. "Ready?" he asked. I nodded, but I didn't feel right like this. He climbed down. A second later the chute door was flung open.

The bull plunged out of the chute and I was in trouble from the first jump. It wasn't because he was bucking all that well. The problem was me. I was out of rhythm with him. It was all wrong.

I hit the dirt—and scrambled to my feet a split second later. Rhino had taught me what happened if you lie around too long. But this bull wasn't a fighter. He was already trotting out the gate Jana was holding open for him.

I brushed the dirt off my clothes and picked up my hat. Head down, I trudged back to

Chase. I could feel his eyes on me, but I wouldn't look at him. Instead, I bent over and tightened a spur strap.

Chase's voice finally broke the silence. "Well, what did you learn from that experience?"

I shrugged and muttered, "I dunno."

"Yes you do. You weren't concentrating. The only way to stay on a bull is to keep your mind right in the middle of him. Then your body will stay there too. Your mind was on how mad you were at me."

I fought back. "I could've rode him—*my* way."

"You might have stayed on him—*your* way. A smart chimpanzee might have stayed on, too. It takes a cowboy to learn to do it right. But I guess you aren't interested." Chase turned and started walking away.

I watched him. Half of me was glad to see him go. Let him find some other sucker to boss around. I didn't need anything from some old, washed-up cowboy.

But the other half of me wasn't so sure. Somewhere, deep down, I had a good idea that Chase was right. I had a lot to learn. And the first thing I had to learn was how to swallow my pride. I started after him.

"Chase?"

He stopped walking. I caught up. "So, uh, can I try another one?" We looked at each other for a few long seconds. "Your way," I added, quietly.

Chase hesitated. Then, slowly, something close to a smile spread across his weathered face. He reached out and laid an arm across my shoulders. "O.K.," he said, "let's go pick one out, cowboy."

CHAPTER 7

The next few weeks went by in a blur. I spent every possible minute down at the arena practising. At least all the practice was doing some good. Chase made it a point to grump and growl at me a lot, but I could see he thought I was improving. He had even let me move up to riding the full-grown bulls. By the end of three weeks I'd tried them all—except one.

I finished unbuckling my spurs after a ride one night and looked up at Chase. "So why won't you let me try him again?" I asked.

Chase knew what I meant. He just gave me a level look. "Cause you aren't ready for Rhino yet."

Getting mad at Chase never did get me anywhere, but I could be a real slow learner. I found myself getting mad again. "Well, when *am* I gonna be ready? Next year?"

Chase shrugged. "Maybe. What are you in such an all-fired hurry about?"

I shrugged back. "Nothin'. I just want to ride him."

That was part of the truth. Enough truth to get by. But I hadn't counted on a little help from Terror, who was hanging around as usual. "Yeah," she put in. "He wants to prove he can do it, 'cause he entered the rodeo two weeks from now."

Chase gave me a sharp look. "That right?" he demanded.

I glared at Terror. I'd been meaning to tell Chase when the time was right. "Yeah," I admitted. "I entered even before you started helping me."

"And what do you figure your mother's gonna say?"

I sighed. That was a real good question. I'd asked myself that about a thousand times. "I don't know," I said. "But she's gonna have to find out sometime."

"Yeah," Chase said. He walked away before I could decide what he was thinking.

With the rodeo getting this close it was on my mind all the time. I could hardly even eat for worrying about it. I was half-heartedly shovelling in my meatloaf one night when Mom came up with the big news. "Guess what?" she said.

"What?" Terror answered, instantly. If my kid sister was a cat, curiosity would have killed her a long time ago.

"Your cousin Becky is getting married."

"Oh, gross," Terror squawked. "Who'd want to marry Becky?" It was one of the few times I could remember when Terror and I agreed. Becky was about three years older than me, but it seemed more like thirty-three. She lived in Edmonton and she always acted like we were some kind of savages because we lived in the country. The few times she had come to visit had been the worst days of my life. I was glad she was getting married. Maybe she'd move to Egypt or someplace.

Mom ignored Terror's comment. "And," she went on, "we're all invited."

"I'm not going," Terror announced instantly.

"Me neither," I added.

Mom sighed and shook her head but she was almost smiling. "I had a feeling that might be the way it was," she said. "Well, I'm not about to drag either one of you, but Becky's my only niece and I'm going. You two will have to look after the chores if you stay home."

"Sure," I said, happy to get off so easy. "When is it?"

"July third."

July third? That had a familiar sound. Suddenly I knew why. July third was the first day of the rodeo. And if Mom was in Edmonton . . . .

I glanced across the table and caught Terror's eye. She winked. Yeah. It was all working out perfect.

With everything falling into place like that I couldn't wait to get in some more practice. I had to wait, though. It was three days later when Jana phoned to say that the coast was clear over at the arena. I think I might have set a speed record driving over there.

When I walked into the arena Chase

already had a bull in the chute. I could hear it banging around before I could see it. Then my eyes adjusted to the dimness of the arena and I saw the big black body. The bull threw up his head and I caught the gleam of a black horn. Just one horn. It was rematch time for me and Rhino. A cold shiver suddenly ran through me.

"He's all ready to go, huh?" I said to Chase.

Chase nodded. "Yeah, he's real ready. Are you?" he added, giving me a close look.

"Sure. Why wouldn't I be?"

"No reason. Let's get this show on the road. We haven't got all day."

"Be careful, Layne," Jana said, looking worried.

"Sure," I said with a grin. "Ain't I always?"

"No," Jana shot back.

I climbed up on the side of the chute to help Chase get the rigging on the bull. One thing was for sure. Rhino was still a chute fighter. He was right in there, tossing his head and banging that one horn against the gate. I wished he would quit. It was getting on my nerves.

There was something else, too. He kept watching me. Even while he was crashing around in there he was watching every move I made. It was like he remembered me. Did he remember how close he'd come to killing me? Was he going to try again?

Chase was talking to me, giving some advice, but I kept tuning out. I was watching Rhino watch me. "Well, come on!" Chase's voice finally came through to me. "Get on him and let's get him outside before he tears the chute down."

"Huh? Oh, yeah, sure," I mumbled. I climbed over the top plank and carefully lowered myself onto Rhino's back. My stomach was doing cartwheels. I settled my weight on the bull and slowly started sliding up on my rope. I could feel the ripple of his muscles under me. I swallowed hard, wishing I had skipped supper. Rhino whipped his head around sideways trying to hook at my leg. He gave a low, threatening bawl. I was sweating.

Chase laid a firm hand on my shoulder. "Layne?" he asked, his voice gentle for him. "You sure you're ready for this?"

I pulled down my hat and took a deep breath. "Yeah," I said, managing to keep my voice level, "I'm sure. Come on, turn him out."

Chase climbed down. He was reaching for the gate rope when Jana's yell stopped him. "Hey, you guys! Dad's truck just came around the corner."

I swore softly as I climbed off the bull and onto the chute fence. I was the only one who knew it was from relief.

"Too bad, kid." Chase was disgusted. "Let's get this bull turned out fast. You and him will have to wait till next time."

"Yeah," I said as I pulled my rope off Rhino. "What a rip-off."

Chase opened the back gate and I watched Rhino trot back into the corral with the other bulls. It was a full hour later when my hands finally stopped shaking.

CHAPTER 8

July third dawned hot and sunny. A perfect rodeo day. I couldn't wait for Mom to get out of the house, but she took her time. I paced around like a caged tiger while she fixed her hair and her nails and her eyelashes. "You're gonna be late, Mom," I nagged.

She laughed at me. "It doesn't take five hours to get to Edmonton even at the speed you think I drive." At last she was headed for the door, but then she stopped and reached into her wallet. She handed me a twenty-dollar bill. "Here, this'll get you and Tara into the rodeo. And it'll give you some left over to take Jana on some midway rides. You kids are going to the rodeo aren't you?"

I nodded without looking her in the eye. *Don't do this to me, Mom,* I thought. *Don't be nice to me when I'm pulling a rotten trick on you.*

"Come on then, Sunshine. Lighten up and take the money. You deserve it for doing all the chores for me." Reluctantly, I took the twenty.

"Bye, Mom," I said.

"Bye, Layne. See you tonight. Tell your sister good-bye for me. She's disappeared somewhere with that Rambo horse. Don't let her break her neck, will you?" Mom jumped into the car and roared off. Feeling guilty, I stuffed the money in my pocket.

When I came outside again Terror was just leading Rambo out of the barn. "Hey, you better put that horse away and get ready if you're comin' with me," I said. "The rodeo starts in an hour."

"I am ready. We just have to load Rambo."

I stared at her. "We have to *what?*"

"You heard me. I entered him in the barrel racing."

"You *what?*" I sputtered. "You entered that crazy horse in the barrel racing without telling Mom? If she knew that she'd wring your neck...."

Terror didn't interrupt me. She let me keep

right on talking—until I'd talked myself in deep. I sighed and added, "Just like she'd wring my neck if she knew what I'm doing."

Terror just smiled. "Ready to load Rambo?" she asked sweetly.

We loaded him. He bit a hole in my sleeve while we were doing it, but at last he was in the trailer. "Get in!" I yelled at Terror. "We're runnin' out of time."

She walked around to the passenger side. Suddenly, I heard her groan. "Oh, no!"

I jumped out of the truck. "Now what?" I yelled. Terror just pointed at the flat tire on the horse trailer.

I slammed my fist against the side of the trailer. "Well, that does it! That really does it! There's no spare and I don't have time to fix that tire. Sorry, Terr. Rambo stays home."

I waited for Terror to explode. But she didn't. She just stood there staring at the ground for a minute. Then she nodded. "O.K., Layne," she said in a real low voice.

As she turned to open the trailer door I saw her wipe her hand across her eyes. I got a real rotten feeling in the pit of my stomach. Terror never cried. She must have wanted this chance real bad. I knew how that felt.

I glanced at the truck. It had the stock racks on it. We had hauled horses in the truck before. "Terr?"

"Yeah?"

"Go lead Rambo up the loading ramp. We'll load him in the truck."

The look on Terror's face was worth the fifteen minutes I was going to lose. I unhitched the trailer and backed the truck up to the ramp.

Rambo had never been hauled in the truck before. He went in easier than I'd expected, but as we started down the lane, he was restless. I could feel him shifting his weight from side to side, making the truck sway. I was glad it was only ten minutes to the rodeo grounds.

I pulled out onto the road, being careful not to turn too sharp and throw the horse off balance. We had driven less than a minute when I saw the red Cutlass in the rear-view mirror. It was Rick Barker, the school's number one party animal. He was with a whole carload of his crazy buddies. I pulled way over to let them pass.

But as he started to go by, Rick leaned on the horn. Heads leaned out all four open windows. "YAHOO!" they all howled.

I felt our whole truck lurch. The outside mirror gave me one glimpse of Rambo's big body rearing to its full height. There was a splintering crash as the horse went over the side of the stock rack.

"No!" I heard Terror's choked gasp. She was piling out of the truck even before I got it stopped.

By the time I got there Terror was kneeling in the ditch beside Rambo. I could see that he was alive. I didn't know if that was good news or bad.

Silently, I knelt beside her. "I'm sorry Terr," I whispered.

This time she really was crying and not trying to hide it. "It wasn't your fault," she said between sobs. "It was those, those . . . ." She ran out of words but I could have filled in plenty for her. Rick and his friends hadn't even stopped.

I took a closer look at Rambo. One front leg was streaming blood. Outside of that I couldn't see any cuts on him. But I didn't know what might be broken. Carefully I ran my hand down the bleeding leg. There was a wicked cut in the muscle above his knee, but I couldn't feel any broken bones. Maybe, just maybe . . . . *No,* I told myself. A horse couldn't take a fall like that and come out of it.

Suddenly, Rambo began to struggle. He threw his head up and tried to get his feet under him. I dragged Terror out of the way of the scrambling hoofs. Then, unbelievably, Rambo was on his feet. He was swaying, kind of drunkenly and not putting any weight on the injured leg. But he was up. He had a chance!

I was running for the truck. "Hang in there, Terr! I'm gonna call the vet."

Ten minutes later the vet was on his way and I was back with Terror and Rambo. The horse was still on his feet. Terror was holding his head as if she could give him the strength he needed. She turned her tear-stained face

toward me. "You go and ride your bull, Layne," she said softly. "Me and Rambo will be O.K. till the vet comes." She really meant it.

I shook my head. "Forget it, Terr. The bull's not important." That was a lie. The bull was real important. But what happened to my kid sister and her horse was a lot more important right now.

The vet took his time going over Rambo. Then he shook his head in amazement. "That's some tough horse you've got there, Tara," he said. "He's got a nasty cut, a lot of bruises, and a pretty fair case of shock. But I can't find anything seriously wrong with him. The leg will take a while to heal, but I'd say he'll live to fight again—maybe even barrel race."

"He ain't called Rambo for nothin'," Terror said proudly. A huge grin of relief spread across her face.

It was almost five o'clock when we finally got Rambo settled in the barn. The rodeo was over for the day and my chance to ride was over for another year.

Then I thought of something else. In a few hours Mom would be home. I'd expected that I'd be in trouble when she found out I'd ridden a bull. Well, I hadn't ridden one and I was still going to be in a whole pile of trouble. I could imagine her reaction when she found out about Rambo. Yeah, as bad as this day had been, it was about to get worse.

The phone rang and I jumped. My nerves were really shot. I reached for it. "Hello?"

It was Mom. "Hi. How's everything with you guys?"

"Fine." This was not the time to tell her. She'd find out soon enough.

"Did you have an exciting afternoon at the rodeo?"

"Yeah, it was pretty exciting." That wasn't a complete lie. The afternoon *had* been pretty exciting.

"Well, Aunt Bonnie really wants me to stay over till tomorrow. You think you kids can manage?"

"Sure, Mom," I said tiredly. "No sweat."

"You're sure everything's O.K.?" Mom asked. A little doubt had crept into her voice.

"Yeah."

"O.K. then. See you sometime tomorrow. Oh, by the way," she added, and I could tell she was grinning. "I gave Becky your love."

I groaned and hung up.

I was warming up a can of beans when Terror came in from about her fiftieth trip to check on Rambo. "Truck comin' up the driveway," she announced.

I looked out the window and saw Jana getting out of the passenger side. I had a pretty good idea who the driver was.

And I was right. Chase. Now, on top of everything else, he was going to rag at me. I couldn't really blame him. He put all that work into teaching me. Then, the first rodeo I enter, I don't show and they turn out my stock.

Terror went to the door. Jana came bursting in first. "Layne, what happened? I was so worried about you. I tried all afternoon to call you, but you weren't in. Why weren't you at the rodeo?"

I sighed and stirred the beans. "It's a long story," I said.

For the first time in my life I was glad when Terror jumped right in and took over the conversation. I felt too lousy about the whole mess to even talk about it.

Terror finally got to the end. "I tried to tell Layne to go, but he wouldn't leave me and Rambo. So, on account of us, he missed his big ride."

I looked up from setting the table, amazed. My kid sister was giving me this admiring look. I'd never seen her give a look like that to anything but horses before. Suddenly, I'd become a hero to my worst enemy? This was pretty weird. But it still didn't change one thing.

Slowly, I turned toward Chase. He'd been real quiet, taking the whole story in. "I'm sorry it turned out this way, Chase," I said, low-voiced. "All the work you did and then my bull gets turned out."

Chase gave me a funny look. "They didn't

turn him out," he said.

"What?" I didn't understand. That's what they did when the rider didn't show. Just let the animal out of the chute. No ride. No refunds. No nothing.

Chase rubbed his chin thoughtfully. "Well, I figured when you weren't there, something had come up. I did some fast talking at the arena and got your ride moved into tomorrow's go-round." He paused and then gave me a searching look. "If you still want it," he added.

If I still wanted it? "All right!" I yelled. I jumped about a metre straight in the air. I was going to ride.

CHAPTER 9

I got to the rodeo grounds early the next day and went straight to the rodeo office. I hadn't slept much last night wondering about which bull I had drawn. Now, the closer I got to finding out, the worse my stomach felt. I stopped just outside the office and took a deep breath. There were a lot of different bulls out there, but only one picture kept flashing through my mind. . . .

I stepped inside, paid my fees and looked at the sheet the secretary gave me. The picture in my mind had been right. A wave of cold swept over me as I read the letters that seemed to stick out bigger than all the rest. RHINO.

I looked up. There was Chase beside me, holding a program. He smiled at me and winked. "Looks like you could be a rich man at the end of the day, huh kid?" he said.

I swallowed and then forced a smile.

"Yeah," I said.

The bull riding wouldn't start for a while, but I got my bag and went behind the chutes to get ready. I got my rope all resined up. And I rubbed in a little glycerin to make it stickier. Then I started doing some warm-ups and stretches to get my muscles loosened up. I wanted to try to burn off some of the nervousness. It seemed to work. I was feeling pretty good by the time they started loading the bulls into the chutes. Then, as I turned to watch, I saw that one big black Brahma hump towering above the rest. It was like an ice-cold fist had clenched in my stomach again.

Chase was watching me. "You still think you're ready for him?"

"Rhino? Sure, why wouldn't I be? Just because I had a little accident that other time doesn't mean anything." Even as I said it, I wondered whether it was Chase I was trying to convince—or myself. "He's just another bull to me."

Chase silently chewed his Copenhagen for a minute. "Yeah," he said at last. "That's what he is if that's what you think he is. Come on, let's go get the rope on him."

I nodded and we walked over toward the chutes. All the way, Chase's words kept echoing through my mind. *". . . if that's what you think he is."* I knew exactly what Chase meant. Rhino was a tough bull. Everybody knew that. And every bull rider was glad to draw the tough ones. That was where the high-point rides came from. As long as I could think of Rhino as just another bull, I'd be O.K.

But, deep down I knew that wasn't what I thought. Each time I looked at that big, black, one-horned devil, I saw the bull that almost killed me.

I rubbed my hands on my jeans, trying to get rid of the sweat on my palms. My stomach felt real weird.

I concentrated hard on helping Chase get the rigging on. That helped my lunch stay put—temporarily at least.

There were a lot of other people around the chutes. Some of them talked to me. I think they wished me luck or something. I answered. I don't know what I said, but I guess it made sense.

The bull riding was starting. The first chute opened. The bull was a spinner. Judges gave high marks for a good spinning bull. The rider stayed with him till the horn sounded. *Eight seconds,* I told myself. *That's not very long. Just last those eight seconds somehow.*

The next rider was out. He lasted two jumps. The bull unloaded him. There was a flash of colour as the clown rushed in. He had to distract the bull, get his attention away from the rider on the ground. It worked. The bull gave an angry snort and charged toward the clown. The clown was ready. He dodged easily aside. The rider was already climbing up the fence. The pick-up men ran the bull out of the arena.

I began to feel a little better. The clown was good. If I did get in trouble, he'd get Rhino away from me. It was going to be all right.

There was one more rider before me. I'd never heard his name before so I figured he must be new. Maybe a kid like me just starting out. One chute away, he got down on his bull and got ready. I was only half looking at him, but something about him bothered me.

Then Chase's voice cut in. "Come on, Layne. Time to get down on your bull."

I eased down on Rhino's back, slid up on my rope and started taking my wraps. The next time I looked up, the other rider was nodding to the gate man. They were outside! The bull bucked high off the ground, landing each time with a jackhammer jerk and twist. I winced just thinking about what that must be doing to the guy's back. He was riding him, though. He was doing O.K.

Come on, I thought, *hang in there!* But right then I saw him start to go off-centre. He was still hanging on, though.

Let go! I thought. *Let go and fall!* But he didn't. And, suddenly, I realized why he didn't. He couldn't. And then I understood what had been bothering me before. He'd used the suicide wrap.

I didn't want to see this. Not again. I'd seen it six years ago and that was enough for a lifetime. But I couldn't quit staring. He was right off the bull now, bouncing along beside it, being jerked up and down like a puppet. Two clowns were working together there now. One was trying to turn the bull toward himself so the other could move in and jerk the rope loose. It wasn't working though. The bull just kept jumping and twisting. I saw one big front hoof come down on the guy's leg, hard. I could have sworn I heard the bone snap, but maybe I imagined it. I was having trouble keeping things straight right then.

"Oh, God, Dad . . . ," I heard myself whisper. I turned my head away and swallowed hard. When I could look again, it was just in time to see the clown pull the rope free. The rider dropped to the ground and lay there motionless.

I could hear the rodeo announcer's voice calming the crowd, ". . . that's the sort of thing we sure hate to see, ladies and gentlemen. Young fellow got banged up pretty bad. But, he's awake and moving down there. He can hear you. Let's give him a big hand and let him know we're all behind him folks. . . ."

Yeah, I thought. *He's alive*. From where I was sitting I could see that. But that didn't say for how long.

The ambulance was leaving now. On with the show. "And coming up in chute number six . . . ."

I could see from Chase's face that he'd been hit hard by what had happened. "Tough luck," he said, shaking his head. Then he took a closer look at me. I guess I must have looked like I was totally freaked. I do know I was shaking all over. "Get off that bull, Layne," Chase ordered. His voice was low, but hard as steel. I just stared at him.

I could hear the announcer's voice. It seemed to be coming from a long way away. ". . . something kind of special today. Layne McQueen, son of Jeff McQueen, who was pretty much of a legend around this part of the country. One thing for sure, if Layne's half the bull rider his dad was, he's got a great future ahead of him. . . ."

I took a couple of deep breaths. "Layne!" Chase yelled in my ear. "You're not ridin' today." I felt his hand dig into my shoulder.

I looked down at the gate man. "Outside!" I yelled.

The gate opened. We were in the arena. Rhino came out of the chute with a high, bone-jarring jump that just about took the fillings out of my teeth. But it shook all the ghosts out of my head, too. All of a sudden, the fear was gone. This *was* just another bull to ride. Chin in. Chest out. Lean back. Pull hard on the rope. Keep your mind in the middle. That was Chase's favourite line. Keep your mind in the middle and that's where the rest of you will be, too.

Rhino was spinning now. How could eight seconds take so long? Come on, who's timing this thing? It's eight seconds, not eight minutes. Rhino stopped spinning to the left—and a split second later he was spinning to the right. I was getting so dizzy I couldn't see straight.

All of a sudden Rhino reversed his spin again. I tried to go with him, but instantly I knew I was too slow. I was cursing myself when I hit the ground. At the same instant the horn sounded to end the ride. I had come *so* close.

But I didn't have time to worry about that.

In my mind, I could feel Rhino's hot breath behind me as I ran for the fence. I hauled myself up on the top rail and looked back. I was just in time to see Rhino hit the barrel the clown had rolled toward him and send it flying. *Better the barrel than me,* I thought, grinning with relief.

Suddenly the grin froze on my face. My mom was running toward me. I took a deep breath and jumped down to meet her.

We stood there staring at each other. It felt like we were the only two people in the whole rodeo grounds. I looked at her white, set face and wondered. Was she going to make good her threat and throw me out for riding? Had the ride been worth the risk?

Mom finally broke the heavy silence. "You had to do it, didn't you Layne?" I couldn't read how she meant it by her tone of voice. I couldn't even decide if she was asking me or telling me.

I swallowed. "Yeah, Mom," I said softly, "I had to." *Please, Mom, understand,* I added silently.

She shook her head. "You're crazy," she

said. Then her voice turned gentle. "As crazy as your dad." She wiped the back of her hand across her eyes, smearing her eye make-up. "I guess that's why I love you just as much."

Suddenly she reached out and gave me a big hug, right there in front of everybody. And it didn't even embarrass me. I didn't care if the whole world knew that was my mom.

The next thing I knew, Jana was there and she was hugging me, too. "You did great," she whispered. I think she almost kissed me, but, wouldn't you know it, right then Terror came charging up. I was afraid she might hug me too, but she pulled herself together and punched me in the arm. "Not bad," she said, "for a guy, that is."

I just stood there grinning like a fool. I mean, I *fell off* the bull and all the women in the world go crazy. I couldn't wait to find out what would happen if I stayed on!

I looked over at the fence where Chase was standing. He just winked.

About the Author

Marilyn Halvorson's life never gets dull. In fact sometimes it gets almost too interesting. Combining teaching high school half-time with looking after a herd of cattle, a collection of horses and cats, and a hyperactive dog isn't easy but it all fits together to help provide the storylines for young adult novels set in the ranching country of Alberta. And as far as finding time for writing, Marilyn always does it somehow. Getting paid for having an overactive imagination is almost too good to be true.

Acknowledgements

The author would like to thank Wes and Chad for all the technical advice.

Series 2000 titles

by William Bell

Death Wind

by Martyn Godfrey

The Last War
More than Weird
In the Time of the Monsters

by John Ibbitson

The Wimp and the Jock
The Wimp and Easy Money

by Paul Kropp

Death Ride
Jo's Search
Not Only Me
Under Cover
Baby Blues

Teacher's Guides are available for
Series 2000 and **Series Canada.**

For more information, write:

Collier Macmillan Canada, Inc.
1200 Eglinton Ave. E., Suite 200
Don Mills, Ontario M3C 3N1
or call:
(416) 449-6030